Short Stories
2022

The Bayside Writers' Group

Published in Australia
Printed by Ingram Spark

Short Stories 2022
Authors: David Mills, Di Motton, Graeme Madigan,
Kaye Nutman, Judith Dowling, Peter Levy,
Sandra G Lanteri, Zhiling Gao

Design: Sharon Hurst

Acknowledgements

I would like to thank all those who took the effort to submit their works to us, especially in these difficult times.

Please note that if anyone would like to make contact with any of the writers in this collection that the best way would be to either post a letter:

The Bayside Writers' Group
22 Stradbroke Avenue
Brighton East, Victoria, Australia 3187

Or email:
baysidewritersgroup@bigpond.com

Contents

Everybody Hurts

As far as Sundays go, this one had been quiet so far. As a crewmember of one of Victoria's ambulance helicopters, I knew that this could change at moment's notice. It did, and on this day, so did many people's lives.

The telephone call from ambulance operations came early in the afternoon. A non-breathing child in one of Melbourne's outer eastern suburbs, a local ambulance was en-route.

Twenty minutes flying time later we were overhead the address and settled the helicopter down in an adjacent paddock. As we made our way through a gap in the property's fence, we caught our first glimpse of the scene awaiting us.

The rear of the house consisted of a large glass sunroom and within it were forty or so people, most of them watching our arrival with a look of urgency etched on their faces. Entering the house, the murmuring of the crowd was interspersed with the sound of several people crying. We moved towards the kitchen area where we could see the local paramedics and a couple of police officers.

On the kitchen bench was a 3-month-old baby boy, James (not his real name). The paramedics were performing CPR and whilst doing this they gave us a brief account of what had occurred. James' parents had invited family and friends over to celebrate the new addition to their family. Shortly after all the guests had arrived, they went to his cot and had found him limp, pale and not breathing. They now stood clutching each other in the kitchen, the mother teary-eyed and shaking, watching a nightmare unfold before them.

Our first action was to have the police clear the room and shortly thereafter forty pairs of eyes were watching our every action from outside the sunroom windows. Moving James onto the floor, we commenced aggressive resuscitation procedures, including directly injecting drugs into his tiny heart, constantly checking for the faintest sign of life. Forty-five minutes later and after utilising every resuscitation trick in the book several times over, we arrived at that point in time that every medical team dreads. The point where the reality is that there is no more you can do. James' short life was over.

As we finished our attempts to give life back to this young boy, I was conscious of a complete silence. I looked at several of the guests, many of them children, faces pressed up against the windows. We had been their hope, descending from the cloudless sky and bringing with us the best of modern drugs and equipment. We were going to save the day and right something that was terribly wrong. We had failed.

I saw the baby's mother collapse into her husband's arms as grief replaced hope. A composed, well-dressed woman, whom I learnt was James' grandmother, came back into the sunroom.

"Is there nothing more you can do?" she asked quietly. The sad reality of the situation explained to her, she had a simple yet moving request.

"May I hold him?" She then wrapped her grandson in a blanket and gently rocked him back and forth, occasionally giving his forehead a light kiss.

Slowly, the other guests filtered back into the house, most of them still in a state of stunned silence. Some went to comfort the grandmother, some to James' parents, some turned and stared out the windows, unable to cope with it all. The police officers, no strangers to tragedy and grief, struggled as much as all of us in that room to overcome the emotional stress of the last hour, the policewoman's eyes glistening with tears that threatened to spill over. Hardly a word was spoken as we gathered our equipment and made our way back to the helicopter.

This was one of the most emotional jobs I encountered in eight years of intensive care ambulance work. Why? The answer I think lies in that this job brought home the reality that a cot death is a terribly emotional experience that affects so many people, and in this case so many people experienced it 'first-hand'. It wasn't a death that they had a comfortable distance from, hearing about it after the event from someone else. They had the sad experience of watching it play out before their eyes.

James' parents, one minute living the joy of new parenthood, suddenly had their world turned upside down. The family and friends, setting out that day to help celebrate a new life, found themselves that night mentally reliving the horrors of an unexpected tragedy. The paramedics and police had one more emotionally stressful event to mentally process and overcome, so they could do it all again the next day if called upon.

And they would be called upon.

David Mills

The Delphi Prophecy

The Temple to Athena at Delphi in the north west of Greece is a must-see of all the ancient Greek sites on the mainland. It sits magnificently perched above the most stunning, rugged gorge with a view down the narrow valley ending in the Gulf of Corinth, a smudge of sea, twinkling grey or blue depending on the weather.

It is here at Delphi that the famous oracle was reputed to foresee the future. Legend has is that the oracle, one of the high priestesses, would breathe in the fumes that came out of the ground in the temple, then enter a trancelike state and answer questions from desperate and needy souls who had traveled hundreds of miles for her wisdom. Reputedly, she was known to utter prophecies that had an uncanny way of coming true.

Husband and I had taken a coach trip to Delphi, urged on by one of our Greek friends to see this wondrous sight and to explore the area. The tour bus had left us in the nearby township the night before and we had settled into a cheap hotel determined to wander the ancient ruins the next day.

The morning started out fine, blue sky and the promise of a few hours of history unfolding before us; quite a joy for a recent graduate with a major in history. Husband was dragged along, mostly a willing companion, kindly reading from the guidebook, pointing out each specific site we encountered. We scrambled over the main sites, admiring the ingenuity of the ancient Greeks whose structures were still standing all these centuries later. Doric and Ionic columns loomed before us, most still standing, others fallen to the ground, left as they had fallen, for hundreds of years, moss growing on the sides of them. Mass tourism had not reached this part of the world and we were free to move throughout the entire ancient precinct, without any guards shouting at us or metal barriers erected to stop our wanderings.

At one point husband came across a small spring flowing from the crumbling wall of one of the temples. He drank from it, then leapt on a nearby rock, spreading his hands, and declaring to the air that he had "drunk from the waters at Delphi and could now predict the future!" I decided not to point out the inaccuracy of his methodology, and to ignore his rather egocentric behaviour.

We came across another couple, two German tourists, who happily chatted with us as we roamed the temple sites. They were indeed very friendly and we shared travel anecdotes and food that we had in our daypacks. We probably spent an hour in their company and felt that we had shared a *simpatico*, an understanding of each other based on the love of travel and adventure. Finally, we parted ways, and began to head towards the nearby town, scrambling over the edges of the ruins to the roadway.

Not long down the road, the weather turned nasty, the clouds that had been gathering while we had toured the site, began to drop their rain and we quickly decided to try our luck at hitching a ride. Thumb out, husband stood resolutely at the verge of the road and tried to look as friendly yet pathetic as possible, hoping to elicit sympathy from a fortunate car owner.

He craned his neck, looking longingly, and then spied a small Peugeot car rounding the bend ahead of us. It slowed down as it approached the two of us. We realized it was the German couple we had befriended and happily expected them to pull over and give us a lift. But to our surprise they hung out their windows and laughed heartily at us our misfortune, sped up and drove away!

We stood dumbfounded for a moment, and then turned towards each other, exclaiming our annoyance and disbelief.

"I hope your bloody wheel falls off!" shouted angry husband, to the back of the fast-disappearing car, feeling humiliation at being snubbed so callously. His Aussie vernacular quite often came to the fore in times of stress! He muttered other obscenities and struggled to pull his jacket hood over his wet head. Both of us were drenched within the next five minutes and pathetically made our way along the side of the road, glancing back every so often, hoping that another car with kinder occupants would offer us a lift.

It wasn't until we had walked for a half hour or so and had encountered the next village that we managed to convince two American G.I.s in a small Volkswagen Beetle, to give us a ride to the outskirts of Athens. Somehow, we felt confident that we could then make our way back to our friend's house, despite that fact that neither of us spoke any Greek at all.

Squashing ourselves in the back of the beetle, we settled in for what we knew from the day before would be a torturous ride. The road had more hairpin bends and narrow turns than a grand prix track. The rocky terrain often created rock falls and spillage across the road, hampering a fast journey.

On the previous day, ascending the mountainous route, the bus driver had sounded his horn as warning to oncoming traffic at nearly every turn in the road.

We tried to strike up a conversation but the American driver was quite reticent, concentrating on his driving. His companion was a touch more talkative and we made small talk about life in Australia versus what we had seen of Greece.

After ten minutes of driving, the traffic slowed to a crawl and there were suddenly police on the side of the road directing cars and lorries around what appeared to be an accident. We peered out the windows, mildly interested in seeing what the fuss was all about. There, in the middle of the road was a wheel of an automobile, lying forlornly. The body of the car was crumpled on the edge of the road, like a wounded beast, injured and dejected. The car, of course, was the Peugeot the German couple had been driving a few hours before.

Both husband and I sat stunned for a moment then craned our necks out the window to check that no one was injured. The German couple was sitting on the edge of the road, looking distressed but unhurt. Husband and I turned to each other and burst into hysterical laughter, rolling around on the back seat. Both the Americans turned to us, gave us puzzled looks and fired a few questions at us.

"What's so funny? Have we missed something here?" The underlying implication seemed to be that we were heartless bastards enjoying other people's misery.

I felt I needed to explain our seemingly callous behaviour. I recounted the snubbing we had encountered from the German couple and quoted the words that husband had uttered.

The G.I.s were suitably taken aback. They inquired as to what our professions were. The information that husband was a theological student who was to be ordained as a minister when we returned to Australia, brought silence. They then offered quite quickly and without any prompting from us, to drive us all the way to our friend's house in the suburb of Nea Smyrna. Clearly, they feared the prospect of another prophecy uttered from the back seat!

Dianne Motton

An Australian Story

Prologue

I wrote this story in March 2012. The story is not taken from any Australian mythology although the names of the deities are from that mythology.

This is a story that I wrote after seeing the ABC documentary "Lake Eyre" produced by the late Paul Lockyer, ABC journalist, who together with his cameraman John Bean and pilot Gary Ticehurst, was killed in a helicopter crash during the filming of the documentary on 18/08/2011. The documentary was shown on Four Corners in March 2012.

I have made up the story as it might have been told had it occurred before white settlement.

If you have seen the ABC documentary you will recognise the chain of events; the ten-year drought, then rain, then dust storms, (The dust reached Sydney and blotted out the sun.) the inundation of Queensland, Northern NSW, Northern Victoria and Central NSW.

How would these events be recorded and told by our indigenous people?

Before we had writing, especially writing of prose, myths and legends relied on oral tradition and oral tradition requires embellishment and repetition to assist memory.

We know this from our own Indo-European myths and legends, and also from the Semitic and Akkadian ones; for example, the Hebrew Bible; 40 days and 40 nights is used to express a long period of time.

A long time ago the land was good and the people were happy;
There was emu and kangaroo;
There was cockatoo and currajong;
The land provided bush tucker;
The young children played in the sun and the billabongs;
There was much laughter;
There were many corroborees;

Then Wala, the solar goddess got angry with Birrahgnooloo, the water god.
Wala had to get up every morning to shine light on the land;
But Birrahgnooloo could rest easy in his humpy and only needed to make rain and floods occasionally.
Wala told Birrahgnooloo not to be so lazy;
Birrahgnooloo became angry and challenged Wala;
But Birrahgnooloo was beaten by Wala, who was much stronger;
So Birrahgnooloo left the land went away to visit his father, the Great Serpent.

Because Birrahgnooloo went away Wala reigned supreme;
Wala reigned supreme for ten times ten moons;
And because Birrahgnooloo had gone away the land became parched;
For ten times ten moons the land dried out;
The emu and kangaroo died;
The cockatoo and currajong went away;
The people became hungry and thirsty;

The creeks, and the billabongs and the waterholes became
dry;

The children could no longer play;

The people wandered far and wide to find water and bush
tucker;

Life was very hard for the people;

So the people danced and implored Birrahgnooloo to
return and water the land;

Many times they danced while the children suffered and
died;

Finally, Birrahgnooloo listened to the people and
returned;

After ten times ten moons Birrahgnooloo poured rain on
the land;

The water wet the land;

The creeks and billabongs became alive again;

They became alive like great serpents;

There was emu and kangaroo again;

There was plenty of bush tucker;

Children could play again;

The people were happy.

But Wala was still angry with Birrahgnooloo for
challenging her;

So Wala burned brighter and harder;

She burned harder and brighter to undo the work of
Birrahgnooloo;

The water that Birrahgnooloo had provided soon dried
up;

The land became parched again;

The bush tucker disappeared;

The emu and kangaroo went away again.

But Wala wanted more revenge on Birrahgnooloo;

Wala also wanted revenge on the people who danced to him;

So Wala called here friend Bellin-Bellin, the wind god;

She asked Bellin-Bellin to show his power;

So Bellin-Bellin blew his wind;

He blew his wind hard, so hard that the land was lifted up.

Suddenly the air was full of red dust like blood;

The dust settled on the people and burnt their skin;

The people could not see or breathe

Bellin-Bellin kept blowing and soon the sun could not be seen;

And the land became dark, like as night

For three days it was night and the sun could not be seen.

Finally, Bellin-Bellin grew tired;

And the wind stopped;

And the sun could be seen again.

But now Birrahgnooloo was angry with Wala and Bellin-Bellin;

Birrahgnooloo raised himself and called the rain.

Birrahgnooloo called for rain to hide the sun and diminish Wala's power over the land.

And so it rained so much that the sun could not be seen during the day;

It rained for many moons, too many moons to be counted;

And the great rivers filled with water and their waters
spread across the land;
And the land was divided into islands;
There was no longer land.

There was no dry place for the emu and the kangaroo;
And there was no dry place for the people to sit;
And all the bush tucker was covered by water;
And the people became hungry;
And the rivers became great torrents;
And people were washed away and were drowned.
And there were no corroborees;
There were would be no corroborees until
Birrahgnooloo stopped being angry with Wala.
So, the people implored Birrahgnooloo to stop the rain.
Birrahgnooloo then saw the suffering of the people;
So Birrahgnooloo relented and stopped the rain;
Eventually the islands became land again;
And the cockatoo and the currajong came back;
And the people were able to eat again;
But many people had gone to the spirit land;
And the corroboree was sad because so many were
missing.

Graeme J Madigan

The Father's Truth

Josie lay awake waiting for sounds to tell her that her father was home. The telephone had rung in the night. She listened to hushed voices. Mr Day had died and her father had been called out.

The shadows in her bedroom seemed longer and greyer. The new day was creeping in pathetically. She placed her arms across her chest, opened her eyes wide, stared at the ceiling and pictured Mr Day lying dead. Flat. She counted to twenty-eight then gasped in new breath. She imagined her father holding the hands of the two Day daughters telling them how fortunate their father was to have had such brave daughters. They would have looked into her own father's eyes and asked why, why? Why indeed! Josie punched her pillow, cross that Mr Day died because he was the only person who let her hand out the hymn books on Sunday.

The Day's daughters had come to the Vicarage just a week before their father died with a basket of plums. Josie wished they'd give their stupid plums to someone else. Her father had looked at the little girls with his kind twinkly eyes, ruffled their ridiculous long curly hair saying he loved plums and thanked them seven times.

"Not true. He doesn't like plums at all," Josie mumbled as she made one of her ugly faces and poked out her tongue.

At around 6.30am he returned to the Vicarage. Josie

crept downstairs and watched as he shuffled papers round his study desk. He dragged off his grey pullover and tied a black vest-front to his chest. He needed another hand to help him.

Josie stood back biting her lip. There were two more ties. He held one between his teeth while he searched at his side for its pair. The ties didn't cross as they should. She bit her lip harder. He craned his neck, fitted his celluloid collar into position then manipulated a stud at the back and ran his fingers around his neck. He grunted, Josie grunted back as she moved from the doorway, out of sight. He didn't look up. He moved to open a cedar box that stood on a bookcase. It was the same box that she had removed a brass key from during the week when she had tried to unlock the secret draw of her mother's wardrobe.

Only once had she seen inside it, the time she was shown a doll wrapped away for many years in faded pink tissue paper. She didn't like it, she didn't want to touch it. It had a China head, large staring eyes that opened and shut and wiry brown hair neither curly nor straight. Four years had passed and she sometimes thought of the 'dead doll'. Now she was curious to know how her eyes worked and whether or not she wore pants.

The little key was too small for the wardrobe's lock and it had fallen to the floor and disappeared underneath it. She had flattened her hand down in the small space between its base and felt for it. She put it out of her mind and now her father, on hands and knees, searched in his study for it. Josie knew that the box contained things that were precious to him, including a supply of Holy Communion wafers which he needed for the 8 o'clock Sunday service that day. He strode heavily into the kitchen and placed a loaf of bread on the table.

She watched as he placed one foot then the other on the back verandah window ledge and polished his shoes while she tinkered with the door latch.

He told her to be quiet. "You'll wake the baby," he said.

At the kitchen sink he scrubbed his hands then bent for a hand towel. He turned his large collection plate hands over and over as he studied his fingernails. Josie watched both him and the loaf of bread. She was hungry but knew not to touch the bread or complain. He cleared the kitchen table, picked up a small toy car, ran his its wheels along his shirt sleeve.

"Broken already," he tutted as he handed it to Josie then waved the backs of his fingers at her.

She sat on a chair at the kitchen doorway, drew her legs up and tucked her toes under her nightdress and twiddled with the car wheels as she watched her father. He thinly sliced the loaf of bread. Josie gritted her teeth with every cut hoping it wouldn't fall apart. He carefully cut the crusts away and, with a rolling pin flattened each slice until it was cardboard thin. He cut each slice into small squares. He emptied a Swallows biscuit tin, lined it with one of her mother's best linen table napkins and using a spatula placed them gently into the biscuit tin and covered them. He looked at Josie as he closed the lid.

"The key," he said. "Have you seen a small brass key?"

Josie shrugged her shoulders twice.

She looked up at the ceiling and said, "Nah"

He strode to his study and placed the tin on his table. He pointed his finger at Josie then the tin saying, "Don't touch."

He was in the laundry bent over the ironing board smoothing creases from his surplice, Josie was out of sight trying out to touch her nose with her tongue.

16

"You'll have a wash," he said jabbing the iron down on into gathers of the surplice.

'You'll have a wash," he said again, louder, as he turned the fabric around.

Josie struggled to turn the tap on at the though. Water came out with a gush and her father leaned over to turn the pressure down.

"Do it properly and quietly please," he said.

She grunted and rubbed her face with a corner of the Velvet soap.

'Properly," he repeated.

She was careful not to cause more splashing and made grunting sounds as she swiped her face dry. Soon the surplice hung from the door like an empty angel.

From her little attic bedroom she watched her father crossing the High Street wearing his black cassock. The surplice, on a coat hanger, ballooned behind him in the wind.

Her little brother was gurgling in his cot. She knew that these sounds would soon become grizzles so she carried him to her bed where she smothered him with kisses until she heard the church bell. On the twelfth toll she placed him into his cot with a crust of bread, his bear and his penguin.

Josie dressed quickly and instead of brushing her hair she stretched the elastic of her school hat. She let the front door slam and raced over to the church clasping handfuls of crusts. The hanging kneeler slapped nastily to the floor. With head bowed she secretly ate, ever mindful of her father's every move.

The walls of the church were pink and beige. It was light, high and airy. Josie liked the way the sun's rays shone through the lead light windows. She was wary of the Holy

Ghost but unlike other churches there were few places where the Holy Ghost could hide. Anyhow if her father was nearby everything would be safe.

He raised his voice. "Almighty God unto whom all hearts be open, all desires known and from whom no secrets are hid . . ."

Josie squeezed her eyes shut. All would be well if she could just get that key from under the wardrobe. The collection plate passed by her. She clinked the coins together. That was her Sunday offering.

Her father held a little square of bread announcing that it was the body of Christ. He had lied to the Day girls about liking plums. Was he lying again? The body of Christ! How could he say such a thing? It was just part of the family's weekend loaf of bread.

The rays of sunlight that had touched his face sallowed to greyness. Even her father had secrets.

Judith Dowling

The Five-Minute Kiss

"Bryant Park Fountain - 2 PM. Come equipped."

The voice sounded mechanical - a computer generated announcement sent to each operative.

Aisling shivered as she slipped her mobile phone onto its charger, pushing an elusive stray hair behind her ear. She felt as though she could hear the ring tone echoing around her bedroom. In the distance, she could hear the news blaring out of the TV.

Da' was likely in his armchair, glued to the screen. He wouldn't have heard the phone ringing, but she had to do some serious deep breathing before the thumping in her chest settled down.

With a sigh, she realised she was again holding her breath. She threw herself backwards onto the bed. Hugging her arms around her body, as the silence hung in the air she realised - she couldn't have said 'No' even if she wanted to.

She was an agent now. Honour bound to carry out the mission.

"Oh, Ash. What are you doing?" she thought.

She curled her legs up onto the faded cover, mulling over what she would do next.

Moving to the wardrobe, she cursed Meagan for assuming she wouldn't need this afternoon off.

"I can't come today. I've already missed one hairdresser's appointment and I can't cancel again," Meagan had blathered on.

"You're always saying you do so little when you go out, anyway..." Ash mimicked.

Why did she always get the blame? The others - her three older sisters - thought they were better because she agreed to stay at home while studying.

Aisling pulled her long coat out, slipping it on. She paused, looking at herself in the mirror. A sheepish smile crossed her lips; the Lucite green enhanced her hair and the chunky suede boots seemed to make her legs look shapely.

"Look ordinary; don't draw attention to yourself," she had been told at the induction.

She pushed her hair up under a sloppy beanie. Much more ordinary looking, she thought. Some wisps of auburn hair peeked out as she nodded with approval at her reflection.

Putting a hand on her father's arm, Aisling felt the dry warmth of his skin and gave it a tender squeeze. He looked up, startled at the sight of her in outdoor gear, his steely blue eyes glowering under his bushy eyebrows.

"I am NOT going out. It's blowing a hooley out there! And there's more snow forecast."

"No Da," she kept her voice low and soothing, "you don't have to go out. I'm just going to meet a friend for a wee while. Remember? I said I might."

She'd said no such thing. She'd been relying on the others, but it was a risk she'd have to take.

With a reassuring smile, she put a plate of biscuits on the little side table, next to the fluorescent juice Da' loved. He eyed her with suspicion. Since the illness had taken hold, he'd become wary of anything out of the ordinary . . . like being left alone.

He slapped her hand away like a petulant child. "Oh, go if you must!"

Rubbing her hand, she felt the sting dissipate. If that was all Da' did, she knew she would make it.

A tear snuck up on her; she resisted the temptation to stomp out of the house, her nerves a-jangle. Taking a few deep breaths, Aisling fleetingly scanned the room for any signs of danger. She ticked his safety list off in her head. Childproof mesh guarded the faux log fire as it cast a fractured glow on the light streaming into the room. The tumbler of squash was plastic. His Velcro slippers were tight on his feet.

Her father gripped the TV remote control in one hand, his blue veins sticking out within the tightness of his hold. As he pursed his lips, his chin wobbled a little, then he turned up the volume another notch, and nestled down into the comfort of his chair, dismissing her.

She didn't like the secrecy.

She had to go. Her mission - their mission - must be accomplished with stealth. Turning on her heel, she pulled a scarf around her neck, then left.

Outside, the chill of the wind hit her. Head down, she pulled the beanie further down over her ears. Looking back, she could see a slight movement of the curtains as her father darted back out of the way. He was faster on his feet than her sisters gave him credit for. As she walked off, she realised her hand was half raised to wave goodbye.

The swirling snow eddied between frost patterned cars sensibly parked up for the day. She walked between them onto a street almost as frozen as the snow itself. Nothing moved.

Ahead of her, the Common lay stretched out in a dazzling white expanse; a frozen tundra belying the games she and her sisters had played there during the soft summer months of their childhood. The far-off trees stood tall, bearing the weight of the last outpouring of snow on bending branches.

Looking ahead, Aisling set her sights on the gates to the walled garden. Her feet flattened the carpet beneath her and left a trail of squeaky indented footsteps. She looked at her toes, grateful for the warmth of her boots. The air around her smelt fresh. There was a haze of breath as she exhaled. The howling wind dropped.

She felt as isolated out there as she sometimes did at home.

"Why are you doing this, Ash?' she asked herself for the umpteenth time. The answer as usual - 'to change things, to make things better.'

"You'd be proud of me Mum," she said out loud, and as an afterthought, looked up to the leaden sky.

She heard crunching footsteps running in her direction. A hand tapped her right shoulder as the owner dodged to the left. She gave a startled cry.

Swirling around, one hand in front of her face and the other grasping the keys in her pocket, she looked at the shiny silver buttons on a heavy green trench coat inches from her nose. Taking a quick step away, she raised her eyes to the bespectacled face of Jack. A huge grin, crinkling the corners of his eyes, lit up his face. Running a hand through his ragged hair, he laughed.

"I thought it was you. Come on, Aisling Doyle, or you'll be late, and we can't have that."

She wondered if he'd been lurking outside the apartment block, waiting for her to come out; seeing if she would uphold her promise. His skin bore a leftover tan, not a red flushed glow as hers must. No crimson nose; even his fingers didn't look blue. He didn't look cold, even with his bare head. If the chilliness of the February day bothered him, she couldn't tell. An old white opera scarf, his trademark at their meetings, shielded his neck from the rough texture of his coat.

"Jack," she breathed at last, regaining the balance of her wobbly turn.

"Miss Doyle." He offered his arm to her for the rest of the journey as they trampled through drifts of deep snow. She slipped her arm through his with a shy smile and felt herself relax a little.

They approached the urban forest at the centre of the Common, watching as other figures arrived, making their way to the isolated garden within. They exchanged few words. Her look was tentative, he raised his eyebrows and smiled at her.

More operatives arrived from all directions. They gathered in small quiet groups, with one or two standing aloof around the edge.

"Perhaps they're guards," she nudged Jack. "They're here to prevent the escape of anyone who has changed their minds." She saw his grin spread wide and returned with her own.

They charged the atmosphere with hushed anticipation as a man with a loudhailer – Chief - put his hand on the ornate fountain's wide edge and stepped up.

"Thank you all for coming out today to be part of our mission."

He surveyed a sea of distinct faces, a maze of different size and age, as he beamed.

"We have here a nice cross-section of society. No one will look out of place. You all look like typical city dwellers."

He stamped his feet a little as if to warm them.

"Agents Smith, Brown, Rodriguez and Lee will be on audio," Chief continued, pointing at each of four people to his right as they moved their lapels and scarves to show hidden microphones.

"Agent Williams will be on video and agent Miller will have her camera on burst mode, continuous picture taking. I will position Williams and Miller on the upper steps at first."

A tall man and woman to his left smiled at the crowd, holding their cameras high.

"No specific instructions, people. You know the aim of the game. Just do what looks natural. Now… synchronise watches."

Over 200 agents looked at their watches, as a frisson of excitement rippled through the crowd.

Jack and Aisling watched as small groups moved across the road from the park. They entered the extensive building with all the innocence of everyday travellers. Some pulled suitcases or carried overnight bags as they wandered round, blending in with the crowds, the dusty sunlight falling at their feet.

Jack held Aisling's hand as they walked through the expansive entrance and half way down the stone steps. They looked towards the clock hanging from the ceiling, its second hand ticking towards the moment they would go into action. Though unsure which of the people were also agents, they recognised a few by the colour of their clothing as they flounced past towards the main concourse. As the minute hand on the clock quivered towards the numeral 6, Jack moved to the step below Aisling and stared into her eyes.

"This is it, Ash," he said, holding her in a warm embrace. Then their lips touched.

Wide eyed, she watched his eyes close and felt a warmth spread through her body, as her nerves disappeared.

The clock's hand hit 2:30 pm. Agent Mac Lee and his colleagues, stationed in several parts of the large hall, swung into action. The immense hall filled with confusion, then hushed.

The casual assistant standing in the Box Office booth froze as she looked around in confusion, feeling alone behind the flimsy counter witnessing what she would later term 'the weirdness'.

Around her, hundreds of people had stopped; freeze framed. The sales girl wasn't sure what to do, so she stepped back, grabbed a rolled-up film poster and held it in her hand like a police baton, as she looked around.

To her right, a young couple stood embracing on the stairs. She watched them. The girl had one toe resting on the step above. Her wide startled eyes looked as if the kiss was a surprise. They were motionless.

A man brushed by Aisling and Jack, saying, "Excuse me.'

His rubber boots made a dull pounding sound as he stepped down the last few stairs past the booth. He noticed something odd, stopped, then backtracked out of the frame of a group of six teenagers taking a photo; one was making bunny ears over the head of his friend, a laugh frozen on his face. Rather than walk through, the man sidled round the photographer, who stayed poised. There was no sound, though their various expressions showed they were shrieking in amusement. With a raised eyebrow, he moved on.

Aisling could see a family of four standing under the clock as it touched on 2:30 p.m. The father looked up, checking the accuracy of his watch. He looked down as his wife gasped. His daughter pinched his sleeve between her fingers. The little girl snuggled into him, thumb in mouth. The wife's head swivelled left and right.

"Cooool!" the young boy said.

He watched papers fly out of a man's attaché case, drifting in an untidy mess across the ground. The frowning man froze, reaching forlornly for the papers.

The boy saw a couple snogging on the stairs. His jaw dropped a little. Turning, he saw a guy standing still like a guardsman on the unmoving 'Down' escalator. A couple behind the man leaned into each other, not moving but smiling and holding hands, calm in the sun's rays.

A group of girls going up the twin escalator nudged and pointed, their bodies twisting round as they giggled and pointed out other 'statues' to each other.

The boy looked at the attendant in the Theatre booth, standing as transfixed as the others, though not as good as the rest. He narrowed his eyes; she swayed as her chest heaved up and down.

Continuing his gazing, he saw a teenage girl in a red hat, yoghurt carton in her hand, spoon midway to her lips. Her friends had frozen likewise, sucking at straws in milk-shake containers with humour in their eyes. His eyes swept over a tall guy, stopped mid-step - heel up, toe down, nose in the air. A tatty black suitcase was stationary on tilted wheels behind him.

Next to the man, a large woman was pulling a coat off; or was it on? The boy's eyes roved, seeing individuals looking at maps and train schedules, stock still in mid glance, captured like a photograph. He smiled in wonder.

Looking back to his family, he saw a couple seeming to argue. Their teeth bared, tongues still, their eyes wild, one finger pointing at the other, but without a sound. Nearby, a girl in a short skirt and tie leaned on a pillar. She held a mobile phone to her ear, her arm wrapped around her waist like she was being hugged. She smiled as her thick

26

lashed eyes looked off into space. The boy wanted to see if she would move. He walked up to her and prized the phone from her grasp. No reaction. The dreamy smile stayed on her lips. With a gentle push, he got it back into her hand and grinned.

"Sooo Coool," he said again, with an admiring shake of his head.

From her vantage point on the stairs, Aisling watched as a cart rounded the corner from the service area. The motor of the sit on sweeper chugged away at its customary 4 mph. The driver stood on the brake and blew the horn. A man in front of him was looking at the ceiling. The driver looked up too, then looked around, seeing no movement anywhere. Creasing his face into a scowl, he beeped again.

"Beep, beep!"

Again, "Beeep – Come on!"

Curious faces turned to him as travellers continued wandering around, but the frozen man wasn't taking any notice. The driver pulled the walkie-talkie from its holster on the dashboard.

"Come in control," he said in his most officious voice.

"There are hundreds of people everywhere." Then, thinking he ought to clarify the situation a little more, he said, "They're not moving and I can't move the cart."

"Beep, beeep!"

"Robbo here; Come in control.'

He scratched his head, then folded his arms over his round belly.

'I can wait as long as you can,' he told the motionless form in front of him, determined not to change his trajectory.

Aisling wondered at his frustration. Would he get out and push the agent out of the way? She sighed as the driver did nothing. She was aware of the warmth of Jack's breath as his nose touched the side of her own.

Agents Williams and Miller moved around, acting like tourists, taking pictures and video. Smith, Brown, Rodriguez and Lee, wandering likewise, were capturing some great audio to edit over the video.

"Do you think it's some kind of protest?" they caught one woman saying to her friend.

"This is crazy; fun but crazy!" another laughed, twirling around. Her eyes bounced off each still life as she span.

"How long has this been happening?" Chief asked the family under the clock.

"A few minutes," the father said. "This guy dropped his papers on the ground and then . . . well, everyone just froze. It's weird as."

"Beeep, beep!" Robbo honked the horn for what felt like the 20th time.

Then, the man staring at the ceiling walked away.

Soon, the typical bustle was back as the frozen tableaux began moving around the space as if nothing had happened.

"Err, it's okay Central. They're moving now."

The whole thing seemed over as soon as it began. Five minutes on the dot. Agents began slipping out of the building as cheering echoed round the hall. The astonished crowd started clapping, and smiling and talking to one another.

"Do you know what's just happened?" Chief said to the Early Booking clerk, passing her on his way to the escalator.

"No idea," she said, with a shake of her head. She stared past him into the hall. "That's some of the craziest stuff I've ever seen, but it's made my day." She offered him the crinkled poster in her hand, but he shook his head with a smile.

Behind him, a still scowling cart driver shook his head as his machine began sweeping up some blank pages left behind on the floor.

In Bryant Park, a large crowd again gathered together by the fountain. While some played piggyback or ran among the trees, others hugged, laughed, and sang.

Aisling and Jack lay in the snow, waving their arms and legs to make snow angels as they stared up at the darkening sky. Neither wanted to end the sense of exuberance and achievement. Ash caught Jack's eye and said, "Thanks, Jack."

Chief again took up his stance on the edge of the frozen fountain to thank everyone.

"Some of you joined us last year . . ." a few people shouted 'YES'.

" . . . and some came to our food court musical in September"... a number shouted, 'WHOOHOO.'

"I'm proud to say that 217 people took part in today's Operation Frozen. We are proud to call you genuine agents," he said with a bow. The crowd let out a cheer, and Jack pulled Aisling closer.

"You can watch the event on the Flash Mob agency website and on YouTube... oh, and there'll be a notice to sign up for further missions."

He beamed as he looked at the crowd, straining above their heads, his eyes lingering here and there. "We're looking for redheads for another secret mission bringing HAPPINESS to this great community of ours. So, see who you can recruit. I thank you all, and wish you a safe journey home."

Hanging back as the crowd dispersed, Aisling and Jack exchanged embarrassed smiles. They had held a five-minute kiss - their first kiss; not something they'd practised in Improv Class. Her brain had been in half a mind to slap him for his impertinence. In reality, she admitted she hadn't minded, and it gave her hope.

Now they were having to say goodbye. Jack pulled off Aisling's black beanie and tousled her long auburn locks, then ran a hand through his own hair.

"You know Ash, I think I can get some red hair dye," he laughed as he nudged her, then leaned forward, his dark blond head touching hers.

Jack took Aisling's hand as they walked through the snow back towards her apartment. Fingers intertwined he led her ever forward, chatting a little, but knowing she had to return to her father.

As Aisling stood on the opposite side of the road to her home, she was overwhelmed with a mixture of feelings; guilt? trepidation? happiness?

Looking up, she saw her da' waving at her from the window. She waved back. He was pointing to something inside the room laughing, clapping, and doing a little jig. The upside of his meds was finding some things hilarious, she remembered thankfully.

They were not to know that the news stations had already picked up the story of the strange events. They displayed parts of the video footage on the three o'clock news, causing wild behaviour in her father. She couldn't know he had stared at the screen, recognising her hat and coat as it panned in on the couple on the stairs. Even without seeing her face, there was that striking red hair peeking out beneath her cap. He'd been flashed back to those same steps, hugging his Bernadette when she'd been a young lass with Titian hair, like her four daughters.

By the time Aisling had said goodbye with a chaste hug, peck to the cheek and agreement to meet later in the week, her father was sitting in his armchair, munching on a biscuit and watching the weather report. It wouldn't be long before his sudden flare of joy would be forgotten. He'd forget his happiness for his daughter, the young one he thought was always getting under his feet.

A day to remember, but only one of them would.

Kaye Nutman

The Removalist

The sitting tenants never extended their lease on 28 Queens Road, meaning that each year like clockwork it went back on the market. Sandra was new to this particular letting agency, but the notes for this property had given her an overview of its history. Unusually, it had been rented out since it was built, sometime in the late 1970s. More than forty years of annual turnover – that level of consistency was remarkable, but no one ever stayed more than a year at 28 Queens Road.

Still learning her way around the new-to-her suburb, Sandra put the address into the maps app. The house sat squat at the end of the street and had been positioned at an odd angle in the plot. It was close to the sewage works at the edge of the old township, built before developers had created modern estates on the other side of town. Sandra scrolled through the condition report photos on her iPad, it was a shitty little house really. The decor was dated, had never been updated, and the rooms were pinched, miserly somehow. No matter, the garden was generous, and the owner hadn't increased the rent for a couple of years – it would be tenanted in days once it was listed again.

The departing tenants were a family of three and Sandra's predecessor had suspicions that they'd been hiding a dog, which was against the terms of their lease, obviously. Sandra had to do the condition report for the owner and whoever the incoming tenants would be. She made a mental note to check for dog damage. She booked the inspection in for Monday, feeling generous. The outgoing family would have a full weekend to make good any damage. Sandra's acrylics tapped on the iPad; she relished the challenge of clawing back the full deposit on a ton of tiny technicalities. Monday was going to be fun.

***

Janie was at sixes and sevens. The house, the hated house, was in complete chaos. Boxes were stacked up in every room, with more waiting to be assembled and taped up. Her partner Ben was out in the garage while their verboten dog Dilbert was racing around the back yard barking and, unhelpfully, it had started to rain. She let Dilbert back in but was too slow to catch him before he trailed muddy pawprints through the house. Why had they thought this place would suit them? It had been a horrible twelve months – too hot in summer, freezing in winter – the 1970s bathroom that had seemed so adorably kitsch when they did the viewing had a strange smell that no amount of ammonia could shift. Although she hated moving with a passion, she'd be glad to see the back of this place. It had been a terrible mistake, but at least it'd be over soon.

Janie sighed again – seriously, sighing seemed to be her default mode ever since they'd moved in – perhaps it was time to tackle the bathroom. She grabbed a couple of the medium-sized tea chest boxes and started bagging up the contents of the bathroom cabinet. Oh god, she'd forgotten! The glass shelf inside the cabinet had snapped in half months ago under the weight of the teenager's hair products. Christ, they'd need to get a new piece of glass cut to size. Janie was counting on getting their deposit back. Six weeks' rent and rent was expensive, even for a shithole like this. She needed to write a list of all the things they still needed to fix.

The problems were falling like dominos, a cascade of problems. Fixing the cabinet required Janie to know the dimensions so that she could get the glass custom cut, but that meant she needed the tape measure and where was that? Probably already in a box somewhere. Opening the boxes to find a tape measure – Janie was sure they had at least three – was needle in haystack territory. The smarter thing would be to simply buy a new tape measure, but she simply didn't have the time to stop what she was doing, also, she wasn't entirely certain at this exact moment where her bag with her wallet was. She found her bag hanging in the hall, but her wallet wasn't in it. It was almost as if their belongings moved of their own volition because nothing was ever where she thought she'd left it. It drove Janie to distraction.

"Hey, Bella! Have you seen my wallet anywhere?"

Bella was sixteen and greeted anything she didn't like – her parents, life in general, but also this house and the whole concept of moving in particular – with truculent silence. Janie knocked on her daughter's bedroom door.

"What?"

"Can I come in? Have you seen my wallet? I need to run to the shops for a few bits."

"No. I have not. Seen. Your. Wallet." Bella's voice was curt and each word was bitten off so that Janie could hear the full stops. Bella's condescension was a wave that washed under the closed door and pooled around Janie's ankles, sending quelling cold all the way up her legs towards her heart.

"Okay, well, never mind." When did Bella become intimidating? Honestly, this year had done bad things for their family dynamics. Ben was barely talking to her; even Dilbert, previously a sweet puppy, had matured into a snappy and recalcitrant dog.

Janie decided to take a shower and at least wash the grime out of her hair before heading down the street to buy a tape measure. Perhaps her wallet would miraculously appear back in her bag by the time she was dressed in clean clothes and ready to go. Janie turned on the tap in the shower to let the hot water come through while she got undressed.

The house watched and waited until Janie was in the shower, eyes closed and shampoo suds in her hair. The bathroom decided to dissolve her, it was for the best. She could run down the drain and disappear. Clean and tidy, the way the house liked things. As far as the bathroom was concerned, Janie had been the worst of this year's inhabitants. Yes, she was the one, the only one, who scrubbed the tiles and at least made an effort to remove mildew from the grout, but she was also the one whose long hair clogged up the plugholes. The bathroom had lost patience, bye bye Janie. The annual spring clean had finally begun.

**

Ben walked from the garage and round to the back of the house through the sliding doors and into the kitchen. He was starving, having spent the last four hours lugging boxes from the house to the garage and ready for putting in the back of the van he'd hired for the move. Tomorrow was going to be a long day. Janie was always useless at moving, easily distracted and ineffectual. Ben was methodical, Janie chaotic. He had no idea why he still put up with her. Perhaps when Bella finished school they'd finally break up – this year had been terrible and if they could have had separate rooms, he'd have shut the door on her without a backward glance. To think, they used to be happy.

The kitchen looked as though a bomb had gone off in it. There were, Ben counted, five open boxes that Janie had half filled, but not finished. Drawers were open and their contents scattered across the worktops.

"Janie, what the hell's going on in here?"

Ben had yelled fit to rouse the dead, but there was no answer.

He banged on Bella's closed, likely locked, door. "Where's your mother disappeared to?"

Bella's voice was muffled by the door, but the sarcasm came through loud and clear.

"How should I know? She was looking for her wallet so, assuming she found it, she must have gone to the shops."

Ben was furious – typical of Janie to skip out when they were up to their eyes with a thousand things still to do. And her sodding dog had scratched the varnish off the floorboards. Ben would need to get some stain and new varnish to repair the damage if they were to stand any chance of getting their deposit back. Ben thought, briefly, about going down to the hardware store now, or he could text Janie since she was already at the shops, but no she'd only come back with the wrong thing. No, he'd have some lunch and then he'd get supplies to sort the floors. It was just one thing after another in this place.

Ben pulled a pizza out of the freezer and set the oven to 200C. The house had been waiting for him patiently. The garage and the house had an agreement about sharing the tenancy spoils, but the house wanted to claim Ben for itself.

While the pizza was cooking, Ben went to the bathroom to wash the grime from the garage off his face and hands. Huh. Well, that was a surprise. It turns out Janie had at

36

least made decent inroads in the bathroom this morning – it looked as though it was immaculate. Ben looked more closely, checking the ghastly metal Venetian blinds for dust, but even here Janie had worked wonders because every slat was spotless. He slid the mirror back on the bathroom cabinet and was surprised to see that Janie had not only removed their toothbrushes and toothpaste – why, woman, why? How were they going to clean their teeth tonight or tomorrow? – she'd also managed to replace the long glass shelf that had broken soon after they moved in.

Ben went to dry his face, but of course there were no towels. Honestly, for each good thing Janie did there were at least three completely idiotically stupid things. Ben stumped back down the hall and into the kitchen. He dried his face on a drying up cloth and peered through the oven's glass door at his pizza's bubbling cheese topping. He really was starving.

The kitchen called dibs on Ben and initiated its annual self-cleaning cycle. He was toast. He was dust and ashes. The kitchen hadn't felt clean all year, coated in a not so thin layer of grease and gunge, but now was its time to shine. An hour later, lemon-scented and sparkling, the kitchen was finally in its happy place.

***

Dilbert started to bark, loud and insistent. No one had remembered to feed him today and now his water bowl had disappeared. He was an undemanding animal for the most part, but surely he deserved food and water? The family used to shower him with treats and pet him constantly, but since he was no longer a puppy all the special treatment had stopped, unlike the barking.

He paced back and forth in the living room. There were boxes in all the rooms, but the living room was the worst because this was the room they were using as a staging post on the way to taking boxes out to the garage. He speculatively took a bite out of the cardboard. It wasn't food, but it tore under his teeth in a way that filled him with joy.

Twenty satisfying minutes later, the living room was filled with cardboard confetti and chaos. Whatever had been boxed up was now scattered from one end of the house to the other. The deep-voiced one had liked those boxes full of little cards and plastic tokens. Dilbert liked those boxes too; he'd especially enjoyed crunching through the plastic tokens and the deep-voiced one wasn't in the house to shout at him. Serves them right for not feeding him. The floorboards shivered under his paws, shook themselves like Dilbert did after a bath or a swim in the sea. Dilbert didn't think to run and anyway there was nowhere to hide.

The floorboards had had a difficult year, far worse than previous years, and had been looking forward to changeover day for months. All those scratches, the claw marks, the mud and, worst of all, when the dog had realized he could get the family's attention by biting slivers of wood out of the planks. It was payback time. The floorboards would simply not put up with being mistreated and walked all over anymore.

Dilbert never knew what hit him, one minute he was racing through the house, barking, and the next? It was so quiet you could hear a pin drop, but the floorboards – respectfully – ask that you don't try it. Their new varnish was barely dry.

***

Bella barely left her bedroom. Not that she liked her room, no, she didn't, but it was where her computer was and, with it, her link to the outside world and her friends. A whole life mediated by a screen and an internet connection.

She was playing Arc Survival Evolved and chatting to the gang in game, that is she would be if her parents managed to leave her alone for five minutes. First Mum had demanded help finding her wallet – like, who was the grown up in this relationship? – and then Dad had expected Bella to have a tracking device that could tell him her mother's exact location. Parents! At least Dilbert had finally stopped barking – someone must have fed him.

Her parents were always their most painful and annoying selves when a house move was in the offing. Bella had decided to pretend it wasn't happening. She knew it was only a matter of time before one of her parents banged on her door again and insisted she start packing up her room and her gaming set, but until that happened she was going to keep playing.

The curtains were closed to stop the sun from shining on her monitor. Bella couldn't remember the last time she'd bothered to open the curtains, let alone the window. The air in the room was stale, smelled of sweat and cheap perfume, but Bella had stopped noticing months ago. Her mother refused to clean up after her now she was sixteen, Bella was supposed to dust and vacuum each week, but since nobody checked up on her she didn't bother. The dust lay thick and undisturbed but the room, in its perpetual shade, was too dark to notice even if Bella had looked, which of course she didn't. Nothing real in the room was nearly as interesting as the virtual world Bella stepped into whenever she was playing online.

It was the bedroom's turn to log off. In the middle of the afternoon, while the sun blazed down on the house's tiled roof, behind the closed curtains Bella's internet access flatlined. Game over.

Unobserved, the house quietly digested its annual celebration meal like a python that has swallowed a crocodile. It would take a few hours to fully assimilate the inhabitants and their belongings, but soon it would be as if they'd never lived here at all, and the house would be ready to receive this year's unwitting guests. Delicious.

***

Sandra was furious. She'd been at 28 Queens Road for three hours and had gone over every room in painstaking detail, practically with a magnifying glass, Sherlock style. There was not a single, solitary thing wrong with it. Not a chip, not a flake, no new cracks inside or out, not a hair out of place. There was barely a mote of dust in the place. It was remarkable. In all of her fifteen years as a letting agent, Sandra had never, not once, returned a full bond to a departing tenant. She hated defeat. Perhaps one last look round would reveal something she'd missed.

Sandra pulled up the photos from the previous year's condition report, holding each one side by side with the place photographed. Photo and reality were identical, indistinguishable. It defied reason. The paintwork was exactly the same – not redone, but not scuffed or faded. The floor looked as though it had never been walked on, in fact, the only signs of life were Sandra's own footprints where she hadn't quite wiped her stilettos clean on the doormat. She shivered, it felt like the floor was resentful and judging her, which was clearly ridiculous.

Sandra gave up. There was nothing. The house was exactly, precisely as it was when the tenants had moved in a year ago. All trace of them had disappeared. It was as if they'd never lived there.

She closed the front door behind her and returned the letting agency's keys to her bag. On the bright side, at least they'd be able to republish the previous year's listing today without waiting for new photography or any minor remedial repairs. Sandra grimaced; 28 Queens Road would have sitting tenants before the week was out.

Lisa Westhaven

Billy

Billy's parent's house was a bit like the old home I grew up in. Federation style with a warm lounge area filled with the trivia and memorabilia of two generations. The obligatory World War Two snaps, various relatives, the three ducks on the wall . . . it was all there. I'm guessing that a lot of houses looked exactly like this. Foreign and yet somehow not!

There was a picture of Billy in a scout's uniform with a ribbon attached to the frame. I stared at it. He was my friend and I should have protected him better.

Billy's mother, Susan Watson, a very good-looking woman with long blond hair, tall and strong-boned, in a nice way. Her eyes were swollen with grief but she managed a smile for me and instantly came and took my hand. She could see I was also grieving.

"Thank you for bringing Billy's body home, Captain," she blurted out.

It was awkward and I simply didn't have a response.

"I'm not sure if I could have coped if he was lost out there."

I felt a little easier. The pain in my chest had lifted. The lump in the back of my throat had gone down. I felt human again.

"Call me Paul please . . . the military is a bit hush-hush on us, as I explained earlier."

Susan smiled, "Sorry, it won't happen again. I just don't like lying to everyone."

"I know," I said. I noticed people of all ages coming into the room and looked enquiringly at Susan.

"School friends that he kept in touch with, and family," she said, anticipating my question.

"Oh! Is there anything I can do for you?" I asked.

It was an innocent enough question but I really didn't want to chat to all and sundry and the funeral, at the gravesite, was another two hours away.

Susan looked up thoughtfully and said quietly, "Actually there is. If you could pick up Billy's ex teacher from the airport and take him to the cemetery, it would be a big help."

"Of course, happy to do it! What's his name and when does his flight come in?" I asked.

"Brendan Willis. In about an hour." Susan fumbled around for a hand scribbled note and passed it on to me. "You have no idea the trouble I had in finding him . . . and then to convince him to come. I arranged for a return ticket to be at the Brisbane airport." I could see tears forming in her eyes. "Billy often spoke of this teacher and I know it would mean a lot for him to be there." She paused to wipe a tear. "He didn't even remember Billy."

I must admit I was a bit confused by it all, but somewhat relieved that I had actually something to do. Stuffing the note in my pocket, and smiling gently at Susan, I headed to the door.

"I'll see you down there," I whispered.

Susan returned the smile and gave a gentle wave. It felt so good to be out of there. The wispy breeze and searing sun were natural restoratives for me and I appreciated the freedom of enjoying them.

Billy's house was in Maylands and very close to the airport, so by the time I'd parked the car and checked the arrivals board, there was a good half hour before the flight came in. I spent them with an icy Swan Lager and a bag of nuts. The lady behind the bar had tried to engage me in a conversation, but my lack of response gave her the message and she left me alone. I was tired and worn out. I kept trying to piece together the scenario of how I actually managed to get Billy's body back to Australia, but it was all a blur. The bits of the jigsaw just wouldn't come together. How could I have forgotten that, I thought. Sweat dripped down my forehead. A fear of losing my mind radiated through my entire being. It was scary.

The half hour went in a flash and I still hadn't come up with any answers re Billy. I'm guessing I was in a state of shock and my mind wasn't computing everything that well. Some things have a habit of disappearing on schedule and I was sort of sure it would all come back to me in a rush - somewhere down the track.

There were about fifty passengers on the flight I was waiting for and, after checking the likely candidates, I had it narrowed down to three. Had to be one of those guys! They all looked like they were meeting someone who hadn't shown as yet. I had to start somewhere, so I got the attention of my favourite in the race and made for him.

"Brendan Willis?" I said, thrusting out a welcoming hand.

"Yes! That's right!" He gave me a nervous smile and a jelly hand shake.

"I thought it was you. But a lucky guess anyway. I'm Paul, friend of Billy."

Willis was about five foot seven of stocky build, glasses and a balding scalp. I picked him to be about mid-thirties, and, from the ring on his finger, a married man.

"You must have been some teacher!" I threw at him as

I ushered him through the lobby to the parking lot. "I'm assuming you have no luggage?"

Brendan Willis gave me a weird look.

"No! No luggage!" he stuttered.

I could see he was itching to tell me something but didn't quite know how to do it. Once he saw he had my undivided attention he suddenly started up.

"I'm not sure I even remember who Billy was," he finally said.

I gave a sort of smile, covering up my own recent loss of memory.

"Is that so? He sure remembered you!" I said.

Brendan continued, "That's just it, I came to Perth on my honeymoon about four years ago. We planned to tour WA for six months, and did that. Our finances didn't quite go as we estimated so I registered as a relief teacher to make some money."

Well he sure had my attention. I wondered where it was heading, and where Billy fitted into the picture.

"I got a call from Mount Lawley Senior High School, to take a class for a week, and I took it."

"Billy's school I presume?" I offered.

"I guess so," he said.

"So what happened during that week?" I asked.

I was getting a little intrigued by it all at this stage.

Brendan gave me a solid glance. "That's just it! Not a lot!" he said.

"There must be more to it than that?" said I trying to figure out what kind of game this guy was playing at. He looked pretty genuine to me though.

We reached the car and I held the door for Brendan, which he appreciated.

"Thanks," he muttered, somewhat deep in thought.

"When I got the phone call to fly over here, it was like some big mystery of mistaken identity . . . or something like that. It made me remember my honeymoon and bits and pieces of the week's teaching."

He paused, to get his thoughts in order, and then continued.

"It wasn't even a week actually. I remember the Friday being a sports day and, even though I was paid for it, the headmaster told me not to bother coming in. So I didn't."

"Anything else about the four days that were significant?" I asked.

"When I got to the classroom on that first Monday morning, those kids, about forty of them, were throwing things and carrying on like a bunch of hooligans. I tried going through their old lessons, quiet chill out time, poetry reading and discussions. Nothing worked. It was one big drag for me, and for them. I dreaded going back each day, really!" He took a big breath. "On the Thursday afternoon, I'd really had enough. I remember I had read about a teacher in The States who devised a class participation exercise, and I gave it a whirl. It actually worked pretty well, from my memory anyway."

We were getting close to the cemetery, but I had to know more that from him.

"And? What sort of exercise?" I asked.

"Oh, I simply wrote a different student's name onto about forty sheets of paper and handed them out. I told the class to write something nice about the person on the top of the sheet and then pass the sheet on for the next person to fill out."

I parked the car and leaned over to Brendan. "So, did they do it OK?"

"Strangely, the class was peaceful for about two solid

hours. It was blissful." He let out a soft chuckle. "The forms were handed back to me and I don't believe I even read any of them. Just sat them on the end of my desk and told the class members to take their own sheet when the bell went. The bell went, they filed past the desk, took their sheet and I can honestly say, I never saw or heard from anyone of that class ever again."

"Until the phone call from Mrs Watson?" I added.

"That's it in a nutshell." He looked genuine enough that there was nothing more he could add to it, so I beckoned him to exit the car.

We walked in silence to the crowded chapel and took our seats at the back. Susan noticed us and smiled. She had her hands full.

I don't believe I heard a single word of the service. My mind was in the jungle of Nam. Going back there was a pressure that would not leave me. How many more boys from my squad would I lose?

We filed out to the gravesite in an orderly manner. It struck me that my friend, Billy, was soon to be covered over with a ton of dirt, and I felt very shivery and cold. It wasn't the first time he'd been buried either.

The priest said a few choice prayers and the casket was slowly lowered into the earthen grave.

Susan, with tears gently flowing, watched in silence and then faced the crowd.

"I never thought I would have to do such a thing. He was a good son, good friend to those that knew and cared for him. And now he's here, forever young and forever loved." She paused and looked deeply into the crowd. "I'd like to thank all of you who are here today. Especially to you Brendan Willis!" She searched for his eyes, which showed sorrow at the occasion and a confusion as to why he was singled out. He could not remember Billy, no matter how hard he tried to. Everyone there were strangers to him.

Susan continued softly. "He often spoke of you." She opened her purse and took out a white sheet of paper. I'd seen that paper before. In Nam! In the hut of Tai! Part of Billy's belongings. Holding up the paper she continued, "This meant the world to Billy, he never went anywhere without it."

Susan saw Brendan's eyes bounce into realization of what it was and he smiled awkwardly back at her. "In his short life, this was the one possession that he truly treasured. Thank you, sir," she said.

Slowly, one by one, the ex-school mates of Billy stood up and waved their white paper as well.

A hush fell on everyone. Susan continued speaking for another ten minutes or so. I never heard any of it. The mystery was finally unravelled. In silence, the crowd started to move away.

I tapped Brendan on the hand. "Wow! That was something! Would you like a lift back to the airport, or somewhere else?" I asked.

He was still in a state of shock, disbelief, awe, pride, you name it, and he was experiencing it.

"The airport would be great, thanks," he muttered. "That's what I love about being a teacher."

"What's that?" I enquired.

"Making a real difference in someone's life."

His words resonated through my mind and I remember thinking as to how fortunate he was to have had that opportunity. I knew I had to try harder and be better . . . to keep *my* boys from needlessly dying. He had my respect.

Peter Levy

Fired

Will stood on the wet steps of Flinders Street Station, head down, shoulders hunched, hands stuffed deep in the pockets of his old duffel coat. He was oblivious to the footy crowds having to dodge around him. He kept hearing the words of his boss firing him. They kept playing, like a dull record, over and over in his head. He'd never suspected a thing. That was the humiliating bit. He'd thought he was doing a good job. He hadn't read the warning signs. If there were any. The other workers were probably still laughing at him for being so dumb.

Absentmindedly, his hand closed over a toy in his pocket. He winced as he remembered playing a game with the boys last night. They were everything to him; the two brightest blessings life had given him. It made him sad to think now he wouldn't be able to buy the bikes he'd promised for their birthdays.

He knew Meg would blame him, as usual, for not trying hard enough. It wasn't true. He always did the best he could, but this had happened before and he dreaded the thought of going home to tell her. He needed time on his own. Some breathing space to think over what he was going to do next for his family to survive. A drink would help. It always did.

Will looked up to see the familiar Young and Jackson pub opposite. He thought of the comforting beers and the sympathetic ears he would find there; the company of strangers who had their own secrets, and would demand nothing of him.

He pulled his hood over his head, ran down the steps, into the rain, thinking only of sharing a few beers. He was so preoccupied he didn't see the red light, and the car coming fast through the intersection. Nor did he hear the screech of brakes until it was too late, and everything went black.

S.G. Lanteri

The Mulberry Tree

Andrew and I moved into our shabby first-floor Art Deco apartment years ago. We love it. In the front garden, outside our windows, there is a gnarled mulberry tree, leaning towards entry. It's old, reasonably rare these days, somehow romantic. It's also untidy, and the brightly stained footpath marks its territory. We love its shiny green leaves stretching towards the building. Rich ruby fruit hang in juicy bunches so close we can almost reach out to taste them.

The whole neighbourhood loves the mulberry tree. It is a landmark, a meeting place, and as an added bonus, it also feeds the street. Freely. It's a place to pause while walking the dog, running fit, wheeling the pram, or delivering the post. Groups of excited school children regularly bring old ice cream containers for their fill of berries. I often watch the elderly who stop. I suppose it reminds them of a time when mulberry trees were in many back yards. Maybe they remember with fondness their mothers' home-made jam, or the childhood song, *Here we go 'round the mulberry bush, the mulberry bush, the mulberry bush, Here we go round the mulberry bush, so early in the morning.* Is that how it goes?

One day I saw a young woman feeding the fruit to her boyfriend. *Try these ones.* I hear her coo. Like a lamb, a young bird, he dutifully, obediently, opened his mouth. I watched this old ritual of love, nurture, power. I'm reminded of much maligned, fictional Eve. Then I saw him screw up his face. *They're too sweet,* he said, *I prefer the others.* Did I imagine

I saw her face fall at his small defiance? Would it be enough to affect their future together?

So much for the humans. Animals also like mulberries. During the day birds, especially large magpies, come daily for a feed. Crows come briefly, black and squawking like petulant children demanding attention. The possums arrive early in the dark night, lightly gliding along the tree's old limbs, and are gone well before the fruit bats, who arrive around 1.00 a.m. like clockwork. The bats are dark shadows, with wide flapping wings, and make ugly, insistent screeching noises, like cats being tortured. For these nights we use our ear plugs. Every living thing takes its turn, not deterred by heat, rain, thunder, or lightening cracking open the sky.

Surprises aren't always good, are they? Yesterday, after visiting the Art Gallery in town, we returned home to find an arborist had nearly cut all our tree down for removal. A crowd of onlookers were visibly horrified at witnessing the drama of its mutilation. Kids were crying, and even the dogs were barking their displeasure. *It was gettin' into the guttering Mate,* he told us, almost apologetically. *The owner said it had to go.* I shrugged my shoulders. What was there left to say? We were powerless, and the damage had already been done. *I reckon the whole street will be disappointed it's gone,* Andrew said, and I know he's right.

Something far deeper than the cutting of a tree has taken place. Nearly a hundred years of nature, nostalgia, tradition, and ritual has vanished, within a few hours, before our eyes. Rain will soon clean the stained footpath, making the tree's annihilation absolute.

Hopefully our mulberry tree will live on in the memories of those carefree kids; those young lovers; the mothers, and the runners, and also in the postman, who, in retirement, may start many a sentence with, *I remember when there was a lovely old mulberry tree on Spruson Street. I always used to look forward to having a good feed.*

The view from our window is now bare. Unshaded. We can freely see the street. The street can freely see us. True, the light is better. brighter, but it's the lost living beauty of nature; the caressing on the window pane by soft green leaves we already miss.

S.G. Lanteri

The Visitor

It is with difficulty they sit me up in bed. The pillows that support my body are plumped up, carefully hiding the stains, and the covers are smoothed over my excuse for a body. All this preparation I must endure for the young man who's coming to see me. Another visitor I'll soon devour with relish.

Every new movement sends pain shooting through me. Especially where the incision is. I pretend not to notice. I do not react. Subterfuge has been my stock-in-trade all my life, and I wouldn't want to let myself down now. I want no pity. Never needed it.

I open my old eyes. Although my vision is not as sharp as it once was, I still have moments of brilliant clarity, so I can see the white uniforms of the nurses as they hover over me, or leave the room for fleeting respites from my requests. There are three of them now because my demands are so great. It amuses me to see them administering to me while gritting their teeth. My hearing, like my memory, has remained excellent. The powerless have no voice, and I have bought these nurses, and the doctors, like all the other silent ones.

The string-bean figure of Joe Miller, the old lawyer I bought years ago, I can visualise even in my sleep. It's always accompanied by the smell of his rotting tobacco breath. He started smoking in primary school, I remember, and no woman has ever presented herself to take him in hand. Then again, I've never smoked, apart from the heroin of course, and look where it's got me.

He's coming at 3 o'clock. This one who lays claim to my fortune. He's just another in a long line of parasites who think they can grab a quick fortune. My fortune. Mostly they are male, these would-be gold diggers, but I seem to remember a particularly attractive young woman years ago who wanted to claim me as her father. To no avail of course. Although there was something familiar about her, I recall, I still took my precautions, gave my orders, and Joe got rid of her as swiftly as the others.

The room feels heavy and airless today. This room, where long ago I loved all those expensive women, is where I now wait to die. But I still have delicious memories of those women, with their bright red lips, their leather, and their whips. Their whispers now caress the air around me and keep me company. Yes, I played my games in this bed I'm now rotting in. I was not stupid though. They were well paid for their services. One in particular was my favourite. I forget her name, but even today I remember the skill of her hands, and her tongue. Yes, they were paid well. Sometimes too generously, and then I had to admonish Joe for such needless generosity. He was always too generous. That's why he's now poor, and my riches ae so vast they cannot be counted.

The injections are coming with increasing frequency now. I've been reunited with my old mate heroin. Its power is working for shorter periods so the dose is getting stronger. Or so I demand. My days follow close upon, and the evenings touch each other lightly. It's only a matter of time now before the great oblivion. The ultimate reality. I have no regrets. Only losers have regrets. I've lived my life on my terms, exactly as I planned it, and I made sure no one got in my way. Thank God my brain is still functioning, still sharp, and I can still give my orders.

The meeting time is closing in. I smile in anticipation.

The deft fingers of the white ghosts smooth down the covers once more. They spray their ghastly lavender oil around me to hide my offensive smells, and brush the few strands of hair that remain on my now pockmarked head. I was always vain, and rightly so. My yearly self-portraits, executed by the best artists in the country, I started after I made my first million at twenty. They hang in my grand entrance hall for all to see, and admire. And, listen, now from the hall, the grandfather clock chimes three. It's music to my ears. I remember winning it from one of my favourite beauties in a card game. Its lines, like hers, were so fine I had to have it.

There is a knock at the door. So, this one is punctual at least. Joe ushers the young bastard in. His name is announced. It means nothing to me. The light is not right and I have trouble seeing him immediately. But I feel the atmosphere change in the room. I wave my hand in his direction. *Come forward* I croak, ready in my last weeks here on earth for some fun at this upstart's expense. The nervous whisperings of the others annoy me. Powerless people never voice their thoughts, but for once I hold my tongue.

The young man swaggers towards my bed with confidence. I hear it. Feel it. Half see it. It's a familiar swagger I can't identify immediately. He appears tall as he leans over my bed, and I can smell his beery, peppermint breath. And something else is also familiar. In a moment I'll put a name to it. I just need a bit of time. And then the clouds clear from my eyes and I understand the whisperings. *Hello Grandad you old goat,* he gloats, *Granny sends her hate,* and I look with horror at a younger version of my own face.

S.G. Lanteri

Geraldine Duck

On the morning of the Prince's Parade Day in the Duck Kingdom the sun is high, and the clouds are thin and wispy, drifting across the soft, clear blue sky. Lake Jade is as flat as if covered with a sheet of emerald fabric. Weeping willows are dispersed along its banks, branches stretching out gracefully on thick trunks trailing into the water like a coquettish, shy maiden, dancing in an imperial court before an emperor. Distant mountains flank the lake on one side with fields on the other distinguished by a large pagoda tree.

Three Mandarin ducks perch on one of the willows. Geraldine, with grey feathers and white rings on her underside and around her eyes, is excited by her new holiday nest overlooking Lake Jade. She is proud of all three of her notable places, especially her nest in the human enclave, where all the high officials reside. Located in a large Toona tree outside the prince's window is a place of great comfort and esteem.

Next to Geraldine is her grandson, Quackie, whose young feathers are still flecked green and blue. His parents and other siblings emigrated to the south. He had been in a precarious situation as a runt, so they left him with his grandparents, and he is happy with them doting on him.

Geraldine's husband, Toutou, which means the top-duck, is, as a matter of fact, only the second-in-command in their flock. Her ambition had anticipated his early promotion. She has high aspirations for him, even though she thinks him a little lackadaisical. The thought of him becoming the top-duck never leaves her mind. She often complains that the real top-duck's wife is always adorned with sparkling diamond jewelry, set in ornate gold. Not to mention her Gucci handbags. The top-duck's wife received all sorts of presents from the lower ranks. At least having a sought-after nest behind the imperial palace would bring Geraldine's dream one step closer.

"The prince is getting more powerful by the day among the people," she often reminds Toutou. 'He can vacate all the positions for ducks like you.'

She and most of her high-minded friends enjoy their lives in the imperial enclave and embrace the prince's policies. There had been some discussion of the latest one, detaining and force-feeding female ducks for two months before roasting them on hooks in the oven. They could accommodate even that because it didn't apply to Mandarin ducks.

"It is ingenious of him to come out with this policy," she says. "Otherwise, his officials would have to receive bribes and embezzle money to keep all of these useless ducks."

Toutou remains unconvinced. "He can't blame the toilet for his own constipation," says Toutou. "Shouldn't he penalize those officials for keeping ducks on the side?"

"Shh," Geraldine's eyes widen. "They'll wring your neck for saying that."

Toutou says nothing, but drops his eyelids.

"Just you wait," says Geraldine. "I have high confidence that our Prince will come out with another brilliant idea to deal with them yet."

Geraldine sees the lake extra green with plenty of algae. Although they have plenty of grain and seed at home,

Quackie has complained that eating grain every day was boring. She knows it would be healthier to have some algae and fish.

"Yay, let's go swimming!" Quackie cheers.

They all jump down into the lake, paddling in the shade of the willow trees. As a gold-medal-level swimmer, Geraldine teaches Quackie how to paddle.

In the meantime, Geraldine gives Quackie a patriotic lecture by saying that the Duck Kingdom is the best place in the universe, where there are beautiful mountains, rivers and lakes.

Toutou shakes his head, looking at her through the corner of his round eyes.

She continues, "Our Prince is making the Duck Kingdom stronger in the world arena. Finally, we can lift our heads up high among the wealthy nations. You'll see how glorious the Prince is on TV tonight at the Parade!"

"I'll be happy as long as he doesn't roast any duck today," says Toutou.

"They roast ducks?" asks Quackie.

Geraldine smiles. "Rest assured! They will never roast us. We are superior. We are a symbol of wedded bliss and fidelity. We are morally upright and faithful."

"Your grandma means we are condemned to have the same wife for our entire lives," mutters Toutou, dipping his red bill in the water and then coming above the water. He whispers, "Apparently, we don't taste as good as white ducks."

"You'll see," says Geraldine with glint in her eyes. "When spring comes, you and your grandpa will have glowing purple feathers on your breasts and black, green, blue crests. We are an array of glorious colours that others can only be envious of." Geraldine continues to impart her wisdom. "You see the weeping willow trees."

Quackie looks at the trees with a blank expression. To him, they are just trees, nothing more.

"Always allow yourself to bend like a willow in the wind."

"That's your grandma's motto," says Toutou slowly.

"It was your great grandfather's epiphany. So you survive well," says Geraldine, looking at Toutou.

"I prefer a pagoda tree," Toutou murmurs. "They are straight and strong." Then, he gazes off into space, a faraway look in his small round eyes. He can't help thinking about his childhood friend's flock being taken away by the prince's people the day before. Just because they visited the harbour and happened to be among the Sea Ducks on the streets so they demanded rights for ducks. It hurts him so bad that he feels as if someone is needling his heart.

"Don't spoil a good swim by overthinking! They are a flock of peasant ducks. There is no shortage of them. Besides, they should have never gone to the protest with those Sea Ducks." Geraldine shakes her head, and her beak opens and closes at a fast pace. "They don't know what good things they already have. They have a lot more rights than we do and still complaining."

"You never know who will be next," says Toutou slowly.

"I miss playing with their ducklings," says Quackie. "Do you know where they went?"

"They went to live on a farm now," says Geraldine.

Then a whiff of roasted Pecan Duck aroma floats in the air and reaches Quackie's nostrils, coming from a nearby restaurant. He sniffs hard with his widened nostrils. His legs wobble with fear underneath water; his whole body shakes like jelly.

"Are they . . ." asks Quackie, a dawning realization comes

to him. "Are they roasting my friends?"

Both Toutou and Geraldine choose to ignore Quackie's question.

'They are celebrating before the parade," says Geraldine.

"I heard some human foreign dignitaries are here. Somehow, they all crave this savage cuisine," says Toutou, fighting back the tears.

Then Geraldine growls. "Let's go home. They must see us watching the Parade."

The ducks waddle towards home in silence, but you still hear their voices. Quackie is worn out after all the swimming. Toutou's heart is still feeling empty, knowing that he will never again see his friends. Geraldine worries about her husband's behavior. As the second-in-command, he needs to toe the line. Any sympathy towards the fallen ones is going to put her family in a dangerous position. They could lose the protection and the privileges they have been enjoying for years.

Once they get back in their grand nest behind the prince's house, Geraldine begins to busy herself with tidying up. Quackie sits down and plays with a yellow toy he has picked up from the ground. Geraldine snatches the toy from him, throwing onto the ground.

"Give it back!" demands Quackie. "I want to play with it."

"Shh," Geraldine puts one of her webbed feet across her pink beak. "The prince's people have banned the chubby yellow rubber duckie."

"But why?" asks Quackie.

"Let him play! No one can see," says Toutou.

Geraldine explains that some bad people use the rubber duckie to insult the prince by indicating his short and stout presence.

"The rubber duckie is our enemy now," Geraldine says. Quackie's tears stream down his cheeks. "There, there, don't cry, there'll be fireworks when the Parade starts."

"Are ducklings allowed to see the fireworks?" Quackie gets excited.

"No," says Geraldine. "But you can watch television through the windows."

"Bend like a willow," says Quackie. "No fun at all."

Geraldine thinks this prince is very thoughtful. He handed out many, many television sets for his people who didn't have one. Who wouldn't be grateful for that? Toutou thinks it is the very act that immobilises his people.

"I guess a TV set makes his people happy," he says.

Then Toutou hears a ping in his ear. In recent years, Say Hello 8A technology enables ducks to communicate with each other telepathically from distant places. So, he puts his little webbed paw on his ear to answer Quackie's father.

Toutou says to his son, "It becomes increasingly difficult to do real work here. Your mother has set her eyes on that promotion, but there is a price. I did a calculation. I won't earn that large sum of money back in just a few years before my retirement without receiving bribes or embezzling money. So, it's no use."

When night falls, the streets of the entire Duck Kingdom are as quiet as the stars in the sky. A servant in the prince's house turns on the television. The prince emerges on parade, standing in an open-top vehicle. Geraldine's whole face lights up. Toutou watches calmly. The prince looks grand and imposing, waving to his soldiers. Geraldine's eyes fill with tears of pride.

"Rubber duckie you're the one! I'm awfully fond of you! Rubber duckie joy of joys . . ." Quackie sings.

"Shhh," shushes Geraldine. "You could be thrown into

the oven!"

Quackie shrinks his neck and crinkles his nose, silent.

Their eyes go back to the television. An extensive collection of chop-chop missiles on tanks cruise by.

"No force can stop the Duck Kingdom from advancing now," says Geraldine, lifting her head up high.

"No need to flex their muscles, if you ask me," Toutou sighs, shaking his head.

The following morning Quackie gets up, waiting for his grain for breakfast. Geraldine gives him some red sorghum and picks up her LV handbag. A human delegation will inspect some high-tech oven that the prince's people imported from a foreign land. Geraldine has organised a small group of ducks to go as well.

"I don't know why you are so keen on those activities," says Toutou. "It's like turkeys voting for Christmas."

"I'm doing it for your sake, protecting your position, and putting our family in the prince's good book for . . ." she trails off.

In the mid-afternoon, the city sky suddenly turns dark, with thunder rolling and a heavy gale blowing, followed by heavy rain. The three of them huddle together in their nest, feeling like it is the end of the world. When daylight returns a short time later, two of the prince's people come to their nest. When they see Toutou, they scoop him away. Quackie stands in a corner, eyes wide open. Geraldine is agitated, waddling around and putting Quackie under her wing. By evening she becomes frighteningly calm, staring into the distance for a long time. Quackie doesn't dare breathe a word and eventually falls asleep.

Geraldine takes Quackie to her sister's nest in a nearby tree.

"I thought they don't put Mandarin Ducks in the oven,"

says Geraldine to her sister, and her beak snaps shut.

"They want potions made from the organs of prestigious ducks which are supposed to stem the high officials' corruption. This is the latest policy."

The rings around Geraldine's eyes become as white as the moon. "Why start with Toutou?"

"He bad-beaked the prince when he spoke with your son on the phone."

Geraldine walks out to the rough sea, holding her head high. She plunges into it and swims straight across the harbour. Sea Ducks welcome her warmly, and together they march onto the streets with placards: Rights for Ducks.

Zhiling Gao